Jingle Bells

W9-CUF-445

Contributing writer
Carolyn Quattrocki

Cover illustration
Linda Graves

Illustrations
Susan Spellman

Louis Weber, C.E.O.
Publications International, Ltd.
7373 North Cicero Avenue
Lincolnwood, Illinois 60646

Manufactured in U.S.A.

8 7 6 5 4 3 2 1

ISBN: 0-7853-1366-4

PUBLICATIONS INTERNATIONAL, LTD.
Candy Cane Books is a trademark of Publications International, Ltd.

Toby was mad. "It isn't fair!" he said as he stomped around the kitchen.

Jeb and Harriet, his older brother and sister, always had all the fun. And tonight they were going out again on a sleigh ride with the older boys and girls from some of the farms nearby. Toby couldn't go along because he was "too little." Would he ever be big enough to do all the things he wanted to do?

Mama shook her head and smiled. "Time for bed," she said. "Maybe next year you'll be big enough to go."

Toby went up to the bedroom he shared with baby Sarah. "Look at how much bigger I am than Sarah. Why do Harriet and Jeb always do fun things together and I get stuck with a baby?" But Mama just hugged Toby. Then she tucked Toby and Sarah under their quilts and kissed them good night.

Just as Toby was closing his eyes, he heard a jingling noise outside. He jumped out of bed and looked out of his window. He was just in time to see Harriet and Jeb climbing into a sleigh pulled by a beautiful, brown horse.

The sleigh was filled with laughing boys and girls. As the Christmas sleigh pulled away from the door of his house, Toby could hear the happy riders begin to sing, "Dashing through the snow, in a one-horse open sleigh..."

The next day was Christmas Eve. Papa called out to Harriet and Jeb, "This morning we must go into the woods and cut down our Christmas tree." Toby wished he could go, too, but Papa said he was "too little."

Toby was so disappointed. Then Mama had an idea! While the others went for the tree, she, Sarah, and Toby made long strings of red cranberries to use as decorations. It wasn't such a bad morning after all.

Just before lunch Papa and Harriet and Jeb came stomping through the house. They were covered with snow, and they were dragging a huge tree behind them.

That afternoon Papa set up the tree in the parlor. The whole family put colored balls and sparkling tinsel on it. Then Toby proudly presented his long strings of cranberries to put on the Christmas tree. He thought his decorations were the prettiest ones of all.

That night Harriet, Jeb, and Toby hung their stockings on the fireplace. They also hung a little striped stocking for baby Sarah, because she was too small to do it herself.

Then Mama said, "Now it's off to bed for Toby and Sarah." Toby thought about begging to stay up later. But he decided not to. After all, tomorrow would be Christmas!

But after Toby was in bed he had barely closed his eyes when Papa and Mama came into the room. "Don't go to sleep quite yet, little ones," Papa said to Toby and Sarah. "Mama, Harriet, Jeb, and I have a big surprise for you."

Mama and Papa wrapped Toby and Sarah in blankets and carried them to the door of their house. There, sitting right in front, was a beautiful sleigh decorated with silvery bells!

The whole family piled into the shiny sleigh. Soon they were speeding through the open fields and hearing the clip-clop of the horse's hooves and the jingling of bells. And as they rode along, they sang:

Dashing through the snow,
  in a one-horse open sleigh,
O'er the fields we go,
  laughing all the way.
Bells on bobtail ring,
  making spirits bright,
What fun it is to ride and
  sing a sleighing song tonight!

Jingle bells, jingle bells,
  jingle all the way.
Oh, what fun it is to ride
  in a one-horse open sleigh!

As they started back toward home, Papa eased the horse down to a slow trot. Toby leaned his tired head against Papa's big shoulder. He smiled up at Papa and whispered, "This is the best Christmas surprise I've ever had."

And as Toby's little eyes drifted
slowly shut, he softly sang to himself,
"Jingle all the way. . ."